A Jolly Holiday Treasury

SCHOLASTIC INC.

New York Toronto London Auckland Sydney
Mexico City New Delhi Hong Kong Buenos Aires

Contents

The Little Match Girl

"Matches for sale. Beautiful bundles of matches for sale . . ."

The young girl looked hopeful as she held out a bundle of matches tied with a red ribbon. Perhaps the people hurrying by would take pity on her and

The Little Match Girl

buy some of her wares. But the passersby barely paid her any mind. After all, it was Christmas Eve, and they had parties to go to, presents to wrap, and trees to trim. They had no time to stop and buy matches from a poor, motherless Little Match Girl.

The Little Match Girl pulled her tattered cape around her shoulders and shivered. The bitter wind blew through the holes in her threadbare dress; the snow seeped through the thin soles of her shoes. The Little Match Girl sighed. If only she could sell a few of her matches. Then she could buy some food for her father and herself. But sadly, she had not sold one bundle of matches all day. She could not go home without any money — not on Christmas Eve! So ever so slowly, she walked on, crying out: "Matches for sale. Beautiful bundles of matches . . ."

Clickety clack . . . Clickety clack . . . The Little Match Girl looked up in surprise. A horsedrawn carriage was coming quickly down the road.

"Out of my way, street urchin!" the driver yelled at the Little Match Girl.

The child leaped out of the way of the oncoming carriage. But her shoes were far too big for her feet, and she tripped and fell — spilling her matches all over the freshly fallen snow. As she crawled around picking them up, two cruel boys grabbed her shoes

The Little Match Girl

and ran off laughing into the night. The poor little girl had no choice but to walk barefoot through the ice and snow.

The snow was falling very hard now, and the Little Match Girl could hardly see. She found herself some shelter in a corner formed by two large buildings. She huddled against the bricks, trying to keep warm. But the bricks were cold, and the ground was wet. The Little Match Girl looked down at her basket of wooden matches.

The Little Match Girl

Perhaps I should light just one match, she thought. *At least I could warm my hands by its flame.* With cold and icy fingers, she took a match from its bundle and struck it.

The little flame flickered at first, and then burst into a glorious pink light. The Little Match Girl looked with surprise at the sight that appeared before her eyes. There was a delicious Christmas din-

ner, laid out on a brilliant white lace tablecloth. The main course was a fat, crispy roast duckling surrounded by sweet candied yams and tart red cranberry sauce. The Little Match Girl had never seen such a splendid meal! But just as she reached out to take just a bit of the tasty duckling, the candle sputtered and went out, taking the sumptuous banquet with it.

Deep inside, the Little Match Girl knew her father would be angry if she came home without matches or money, but she could not think about that now. Instead, she took another match from the bundle and struck it. Within an instant, the tiny flame burst into a bright green haze. In the center of the haze was the most beautiful Christmas tree The Little Match Girl had ever seen. The large fir was trimmed with silver, sparkly tinsel. Red and green ornaments hung from every branch, and a hundred candles glowed into the night. Quickly, the Little Match Girl moved toward the candles. But just as quickly, the match sputtered and died out, leaving the Little Match Girl cold and alone once more.

Once again, the child lit a match. And this time she saw the greatest sight of all — her beloved grandmother who had left her and gone to heaven two Christmases before. Frantically, the shivering

The Little Match Girl

child reached out to the old woman. "Oh, Grandmother," she called out. "You look so warm and lovely. And I have missed you so. Please, do not leave me."

The child reached into her basket once more. *Perhaps if I light all of the matches,* she thought, *my grandmother will keep me warm for the night.* And with that, she lit all of her matches, one by one.

When she got to the last match, she cried out. "Take me with you, Grandmother. Take me where it

The Little Match Girl

is warm and peaceful. But hurry — this last match will soon die out and I shall never see you again."

The old woman swept her granddaughter up in her arms. In a light as bright as ten thousand matches, they soared together up to heaven. The angels greeted them with open arms, wrapping the child's shivering body in warm, woolen fleece. Never again would the poor child be hungry or cold. Now she was home — safe with her grandmother and the angels.

Babes in Toyland

"Come, children! Gather 'round! Help me prepare the village square!" called Mother Goose. Her children raced from all directions.

Jack and Jill came down from the hill. Little Miss Muffett jumped up from her tuffet. Little Bo Peep stopped counting her sheep. Their other brothers and sisters came running, too.

It was the day before Christmas Eve. The children were very excited. They all wanted to help decorate Mother Goose Village for their favorite holiday.

Some children hung garlands of holly and berries on the tall Christmas tree.

Others hammered green, red, and gold wreaths on doors.

And some placed small wooden toys on the branches of the tree. What better way for Mother Goose Village, the largest town in Toyland, to celebrate Christmas than with tiny toys!

Babes in Toyland

Contrary Mary, Mother Goose's oldest daughter, placed a bright start at the top of the tree. This was an extra-special time for her. On Christmas Day, she would marry her true love, Tom Piper. Mary's smile matched the brightness of the star.

But just as she was on her way down from the ladder, a dark cloud seemed to cover the village square. Everyone gasped . . .

It was Barnaby, the richest, greediest, and most powerful man in Toyland. He was very unhappy. He

did not want Mary to marry Tom. He wanted to marry her himself!

Barnaby had a plan, and he was about to put it into action.

"Clear the square!" bellowed Barnaby. "Christmas will *not* be celebrated this year! Take down these decorations."

Barnaby turned to Mother Goose and said, "As of today, I am charging you double your rent."

Mother Goose could not believe her ears. Then Barnaby said, "But maybe we can make a deal. Call off the wedding and you can live here rent free!"

"Tom and Mary love each other," said Mother Goose. "We can't stop their wedding."

Babes in Toyland

Barnaby turned away muttering, "We'll see about that!"

Barnaby's sidekick, Roderigo, found Barnaby as he was walking home. "I took care of everything," said Roderigo. "We'll get rid of Tom tonight."

Mary heard Roderigo and Barnaby talking, and she stopped them.

"What are you planning to do to Tom?" she demanded.

"My only plans are the plans for our wedding," Barnaby said slyly.

Babes in Toyland

Mary wanted to get far away from these two men. She wanted to find Tom. She ran and ran without looking where she was going. The news that Mary had run away spread quickly. It even reached Tom.

Mary did not know that Barnaby and Roderigo came after her. They followed her into the deepest, darkest, and most dangerous place in all of Toyland — the Forest of No Return!

Soon the forest worked its spell on all of them, and they fell fast asleep. As they slept, gigantic spiders came out of hiding. The spiders spun silken webs tightly around each of them.

As the spiders scurried away, Tom entered the forest looking for Mary. He gasped when he saw her. Tom knelt beside Mary and gently brushed a moth from her shoulder.

Babes in Toyland

Suddenly the moth fluttered its wings and changed into a beautiful butterfly. It untangled the spiderweb and lifted both Tom and Mary onto its back. Then it carried them safely out of the Forest of No Return to the doorstep of the Toymaker.

Inside the Toymaker's shop, the Toymaker and his assistant, Grumio, were busy indeed. They had to make all the Christmas toys for the boys and girls of Toyland. These two loved to tinker. Right now they were busy working on a machine that could bring toys to life!

Grumio flipped the power strip on. The great machine sputtered. A large doll came down the assembly line. Smoke was pouring out of it.

Babes in Toyland

The Toymaker scratched his head. "If at first you don't succeed, Grumio, try, try again!"

Just then Mary and Tom raced through the workshop.

Grumio was joyous. "Look! Our dolls *are* coming to life!" he said.

Mary pleaded with the Toymaker. "Won't you help us? Old Barnaby is spreading unhappiness everywhere. He's trying to stop the village Christmas celebration and our wedding!"

The wise old Toymaker said, "Don't worry! Nothing bad can happen to you here. Now, pretend you are my dolls and line up with the other toys."

Babes in Toyland

Tom and Mary did what the Toymaker told them to do.

At that moment, Barnaby and Roderigo burst into the Toymaker's workshop. "I know Tom and Mary are here," Barnaby shouted. "Where are they?" Then the toy machine caught his eye.

"What have we here?" asked Barnaby, walking toward the Toymaker's machine.

Babes in Toyland

The Toymaker answered, "This machine makes toys!"

"Then I will make lots of toys for myself," Barnaby said with a greedy smile. He began flicking switches and turning knobs.

Suddenly toys came off in all directions — and they were coming to life! The Toymaker's machine was working after all!

"Now is your chance!" whispered the Toymaker

Babes in Toyland

to Tom and Mary. "Lead the toys and scare Barnaby and Roderigo away."

And that is just what they did! Barnaby couldn't believe that the toys were alive. When he saw them marching toward him, he screamed and ran. Barnaby and Roderigo ran until they reached the edge of Toyland. As they crossed the border, Tom, Mary, and all the toys began to cheer, for everyone knows that once you pass the borders of Toyland, you can never return again.

Tom and Mary went back to the workshop, and all

of the toys followed. One by one, they became real toys again.

Tom and Mary hugged the Toymaker and thanked him. He gave them lots of toys to take back for the children in Mother Goose Village.

Then he said, "Have a very Merry Christmas! Always keep love in your heart."

Finally it was Christmas Day. Tom and Mary's wedding was beautiful.

And all the children had a wonderful time celebrating Christmas in Mother Goose Village!

The Twelve Days of Christmas

On the first day of Christmas, my true love gave to me, a partridge in a pear tree.

On the second day of Christmas, my true love gave to me, two turtle doves, and a partridge in a pear tree.

The Twelve Days of Christmas

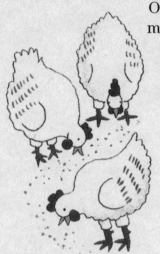

On the third day of Christmas, my true love gave to me, three French hens, two turtle doves, and a partridge in a pear tree.

On the fourth day of Christmas, my true love gave to me, four calling birds, three French hens, two turtle doves, and a partridge in a pear tree.

The Twelve Days of Christmas

On the fifth day of Christmas, my true love gave to me, five golden rings! four calling birds, three French hens, two turtle doves, and a partridge in a pear tree.

On the sixth day of Christmas, my true love gave to me, six geese-a-laying, five golden rings! four calling birds, three French hens, two turtle doves, and a partridge in a pear tree.

The Twelve Days of Christmas

On the seventh day of Christmas, my true love gave to me, seven swans-a-swimming, six geese-a-laying, five golden rings! four calling birds, three French hens, two turtle doves, and a partridge in a pear tree.

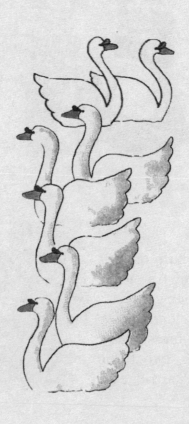

The Twelve Days of Christmas

On the eighth day of Christmas, my true love gave to me, eight maids-a-milking, seven swans-a-swimming, six geese-a-laying, five golden rings! four calling birds, three French hens, two turtle doves, and a partridge in a pear tree.

On the ninth day of Christmas, my true love gave to me, nine ladies dancing, eight maids-a-milking, seven swans-a-swimming, six geese-a-laying, five golden rings! four calling birds, three French hens, two turtle doves, and a partridge in a pear tree.

The Twelve Days of Christmas

On the tenth day of Christmas, my true love gave to me, ten lords-a-leaping, nine ladies dancing, eight maids-a-milking, seven swans-a-swimming, six geese-a-laying, five golden rings! four calling birds, three French hens, two turtle doves, and a partridge in a pear tree.

The Twelve Days of Christmas

On the eleventh day of Christmas, my true love gave to me, eleven pipers piping, ten lords-a-leaping, nine ladies dancing, eight maids-a-milking, seven swans-a-swimming, six geese-a-laying, five golden rings! four calling birds, three French hens, two turtle doves, and a partridge in a pear tree.

The Twelve Days of Christmas

On the twelfth day of Christmas, my true love gave to me, twelve drummers drumming, eleven pipers piping, ten lords-a-leaping, nine ladies

The Twelve Days of Christmas

dancing, eight maids-a-milking, seven swans-a-swimming, six geese-a-laying, five golden rings! four calling birds, three French hens, two turtle doves, and a partridge in a pear tree.

The Night Before Christmas

'Twas the night before Christmas, when all through the house,
Not a creature was stirring, not even a mouse;
The stockings were hung by the chimney with care,
In hopes that St. Nicholas soon would be there;

The Night Before Christmas

The children were nestled all snug in their beds,
   While visions of sugarplums danced in their heads;
And Mama in her 'kerchief, and I in my cap,
   Had just settled our brains for a long winter's nap;
When out on the lawn there arose such a clatter,
   I sprang from my bed to see what was the matter.

Away to the window I flew like a flash,
   Tore open the shutters and threw up the sash.
The moon on the breast of the new-fallen snow,
   Gave the lustre of midday to objects below,
When, what to my wondering eyes should appear,
   But a miniature sleigh, and eight tiny reindeer,
With a little old driver, so lively and quick,
   I knew in a moment it must be St. Nick.

The Night Before Christmas

More rapid than eagles his coursers they came,
   And he whistled, and shouted, and called them by
      name:
"Now *Dasher*! Now *Dancer*! Now *Prancer* and *Vixen*!
   On, *Comet*! On, *Cupid*! On, *Donner* and *Blitzen*!
To the top of the porch! To the top of the wall!
   Now dash away! Dash away! Dash away all!"
As dry leaves that before the wild hurricane fly,
   When they meet with an obstacle, mount to the sky;
So up to the housetop the coursers they flew,
   With the sleigh full of toys, and St. Nicholas, too.
And then in a twinkling, I heard on the roof,
   The prancing and pawing of each little hoof —

The Night Before Christmas

As I drew in my head and was turning around,
Down the chimney St. Nicholas came with a
bound.
He was dressed all in fur, from his head to his foot,
And his clothes were all tarnished with ashes and
soot;
A bundle of toys he had flung on his back,
And he looked like a peddler just opening his pack.

The Night Before Christmas

His eyes — how they twinkled! His dimples, how
   merry!
  His cheeks were like roses, his nose like a cherry!
His droll little mouth was drawn up like a bow,
  And the beard of his chin was as white as the snow;
The stump of a pipe he held tight in his teeth,
  And the smoke it encircled his head like a wreath;
He had a broad face and a little round belly,
  That shook when he laughed, like a bowl full of
   jelly.
He was chubby and plump, a right jolly old elf,
  And I laughed when I saw him, in spite of myself,

The Night Before Christmas

A wink of his eye and a twist of his head,
Soon gave me to know I had nothing to dread;
He spoke not a word, but went straight to his work,
And filled all the stockings; then turned with a
jerk,
And laying his finger aside of his nose,
And giving a nod, up the chimney he rose;
He sprang to his sleigh, to his team gave a whistle,
And away they all flew like the down of a thistle.
But I heard him exclaim, ere he drove out of sight,
"Happy Christmas to all. And to all a good night."

Santa's Christmas
Surprise

It was Christmas Eve at the North Pole. The elves hurried to finish the toys. They put trucks and trains, bikes and balls, and all kinds of dolls into Santa's big pack.

Santa checked his list for the last time. "Good work," he said to the elves. "It's almost time for me to go!"

Santa's Christmas Surprise

Santa put on his bright red suit and his warm boots. The elves polished the sleigh and hitched up the reindeer.

"One, two, three — four, five, six," counted Santa. "Where are Dasher and Dancer?"

"They're still in the stable," said the biggest elf, with a twinkle in his eye.

Santa opened the door of the stable. Then he stopped and stared.

"Ho-ho-ho!" Santa laughed. "Here's a real Christmas surprise — a new baby reindeer!"

Santa's Christmas Surprise

The elves gathered around the baby.

"What's her name, Santa?" asked the smallest elf.

"She was born on Christmas Eve," said Santa. "Let's call her Eve!"

Soon all eight reindeer were hitched up, and Santa's sleigh was flying across the starry sky. The elves waved good-bye.

"We'll be back in time for Christmas," called Santa. He looked down at the stable and smiled.

Little Eve was the best Christmas surprise ever!

Deck the Halls

Deck the halls with boughs of holly,
Fa, la, la, la, la,
La, la, la, la.

Deck the Halls

'Tis the season to be jolly,
Fa, la, la, la, la,
La, la, la, la.

Don we now our gay apparel,
Fa, la, la, la, la,
La, la, la, la.

Troll the ancient Yuletide carol,
Fa, la, la, la, la,
La, la, la, la.

From

Santa Paws

A poor stray dog wanders into town one Christmas season and wherever he goes, he seems to help people. He helps an old woman who has fallen and broken her hip, and he saves a little boy from drowning in a mall fountain. Everyone calls the heroic dog Santa Paws, but all he wants is a home and a family to love him. Siblings Gregory and Patricia want to bring him home — if they can find him.

Gregory and Oscar met on the school playground at ten-thirty. Patricia had insisted on coming along, too. Since the food was gone and the towels in the cardboard box were rumpled, they knew that the dog had been there. But he was gone now — and they had no way of knowing if he would ever come back.

"Where does he *go* every day?" Gregory asked, frustrated. "Doesn't he want us to find him?"

Oscar shrugged as he opened a brand-new can of Alpo stew. "He's off doing hero stuff, probably."

Patricia didn't like to see the towels looking so messy. She bent down to refold them. "You know, that was really something at the mall," she remarked. "I've never seen a dog do anything like that before."

"He's not just any dog," Gregory said proudly.

Patricia nodded. For once, her brother was right.

Santa Paws

"I have to say, it was pretty cool." She reached into the open Milk-Bone box. "How many should I leave him?"

"Three," Gregory told her. "In a nice, neat row."

"Since it's Christmas Eve, let's give him four," Oscar suggested.

"Sounds good," Patricia said, and took out four biscuits.

When they were done, they sat down on a wool blanket Oscar had brought. It was much more pleasant than sitting in the cold snow. Mrs. Callahan had packed them a picnic lunch, too.

So they spent the next couple of hours eating sandwiches, drinking out of juice boxes, and playing cards. Patricia hated Hearts, so mostly they played inept poker.

"Is this going to get any more interesting?" Patricia asked at one point.

Gregory and Oscar shook their heads.

"Great," Patricia said grumpily. Then she slouched down to deal another hand of cards. "Aces wild, boys. Place your bets."

They waited and waited, but the dog never showed up. They had stayed so long that the batteries in Gregory's portable tape deck were running down.

"Is it okay if we go now?" Patricia asked. "I'm *really* tired of playing cards."

"Me, too," Oscar confessed.

"We might as well," Gregory said with a sigh. He was pretty sick of cards, too. "I don't think he's coming." He reached for a small plastic bag and started collecting all of their trash. "Do you think Mom and Dad would let us come here at night? Maybe we'd find him here, asleep."

"They wouldn't let us come *alone*," Patricia said. "But if we asked really nicely, they might come with us. I mean, they're the ones who are always telling us to be kind to animals, right?"

Gregory nodded. His parents had always *stressed* the importance of being kind to animals.

"You should write down what you're going to say first," Oscar advised them. He never really liked to leave things to chance. In the Cub Scouts, he had learned a lot about being prepared. "That way, you can practice how you're going to do it. Work out all the bugs."

"Let me write it," Patricia told her brother. "I have a bigger vocabulary."

Gregory just shrugged. All he wanted to do was find the dog — one way or another.

Santa Paws

He was beginning to be afraid that the dog didn't *want* to be found.

Hours passed before the dog regained consciousness. It was well past midnight, and the woods were pitch-black. His shoulder had stiffened so much that at first, he couldn't get up. But finally, he staggered to his feet. He wanted to lie right back down, but he made himself stay up.

He stood there, swaying. He felt dizzy and sick. What he wanted right now, more than anything, was to be inside that warm cardboard box, sleeping on those soft towels that smelled so clean and fresh.

He limped out to the road, whimpering every time his bad leg hit the ground. The bleeding had stopped, but now that he was moving around, it started up again.

The only way he was going to make it back to the school was if he put one foot after the other. He limped painfully up the road, staring down at his front paws the whole way. One step. Two. Three. Four. It was hard work.

Whenever possible, he took shortcuts. He cut through alleys, and parking lots, and backyards. The lights were off all over town. People were sound asleep, dreaming about Christmas morning. The dog just staggered along, putting one foot in front of the other. Over and over.

He was plodding through someone's front yard when he felt the hair on his back rise. Oh, now what? He was *too tired*. But — he smelled smoke! Even though he was dizzy, he lifted his head to sniff the air. Where was it coming from?

He followed the trail across several yards and up to a yellow two-story house. Smoke was billowing out through a crack in the living room window. Someone had left the Christmas tree lights on, and the tree had ignited! The lights were snapping and popping, and the ornaments were bursting into flames. He could hear the crackle of electricity, and smell the smoke getting stronger.

The house was on fire!

He lurched up the front steps and onto the porch. He was too weak to paw on the door, but he *could* still bark. He threw his head back and howled into the silent night. He barked and barked until the other dogs in the neighborhood woke up and started joining in. Soon, there were dogs howling and yapping everywhere.

After a few minutes of that, lights started going on in houses up and down the block. The dog was losing strength, but he kept barking. Why didn't the people come outside? Didn't they know that their house was burning?

The living room windows were getting black from the smoke, as the fire spread. Why wouldn't the people wake up? Maybe he was going to have to go in and *get* them. But how?

He started throwing his body feebly against the front door, but it wouldn't budge. Why couldn't the people hear him barking? Where were they? If they didn't wake up soon, they might die from the smoke!

The dog limped to the farthest end of the porch, trying to gather up all of his strength. Then he raced towards the living room window and threw himself into the glass at full speed. The window shattered and he landed in the middle of the burning room. He was covered with little shards of glass, but he didn't have time to shake them off. He had to go find the family! The floor was very hot, and he burned the bottom of his paws as he ran across the room. It was scary in here!

The doorway was blocked by fire, but he launched himself up into the air and soared through the flames. He could smell burned fur where his coat had been singed, but he ignored that and limped up the stairs as fast as he could. He kept barking and howling the entire way, trying to sound the alarm. A burning ember had fallen onto his back and he yelped when he felt the pain, but then he just went back to barking.

A man came stumbling out of the master bedroom in a pair of flannel pajamas. It was Mr. Brown, who lived in the house with his wife and two daughters, and he was weak from smoke inhalation.

"Wh-what's going on?" Mr. Brown mumbled. "It's the middle of the —"

The dog barked, and tugged at his pajama leg with his teeth, trying to pull him down the stairs.

Mr. Brown saw the flames downstairs and gasped. "Fire!" he yelled, and ran into his children's bedroom. "Wake up, everyone! The house is on fire!"

The dog ran into the master bedroom, barking as loudly as he could until Mrs. Brown groggily climbed out of bed. She was coughing from the smoke, and seemed very confused. The dog barked, and nudged her towards the door.

Mr. Brown rushed down the stairs with his two sleepy children and a squirming Siamese cat, and then went back for his wife. By now, she was only steps behind him, carrying a cage full of gerbils.

The dog was exhausted, but he kept barking until they were all safely outside. Once he was sure the house was empty, he staggered out to the yard, his lungs and eyes hurting from the thick smoke. He sank down in the snow, coughing and gagging and quivering from fear.

One of the neighbors had called 911, and the first fire engine was just arriving. The firefighters leaped out, carrying various pieces of equipment and grabbing lengths of hose. By now, the fire had spread from the living room to the dining room.

"Is anyone still in there?" the engine company lieutenant yelled.

"No," Mrs. Brown answered, coughing from the smoke she had inhaled. "It's okay! We all got out."

Because they had been called only a minute or two after the fire started, the fire department was able to put the fire out quickly. Although the living room and dining room were destroyed, the rest of the house had been saved. Instead of losing everything, including their lives, the Browns would still have a place to live.

During all of this, the dog had limped over to the nearest bush. He crawled underneath it as far as he could go. Then he collapsed in exhaustion. His injured shoulder was throbbing, he was still gagging, and all he could smell was smoke. His paws hurt, and he licked at the pads, trying to get rid of the burning sensation. They hurt so much that he couldn't stop whimpering. His back was stinging from where the ember had hit it, and he had lots of new cuts from leaping through the glass. He huddled into a small ball, whimpering to himself. He had never been in so much pain in his life.

While the other firefighters checked to make sure that the fire was completely out, the chief went over to interview Mr. and Mrs. Brown. The Oceanport Fire Department was staffed by volunteers, and Fire Chief Jefferson had run the department for many years.

"How did you get out?" Chief Jefferson asked, holding an incident report form and a ballpoint pen. "Did your smoke detector wake you up?"

Mr. and Mrs. Brown exchanged embarrassed glances.

"We, um, kind of took the battery out a few days ago," Mr. Brown mumbled. "See, the remote control went dead, and . . ." His voice trailed off.

"We were going to get another battery for the smoke detector," Mrs. Brown said, coming to his defense. "But, with the holidays and all, we just —"

"Hadn't gotten around to it yet," Chief Jefferson finished the sentence for her.

The Browns nodded, and looked embarrassed.

Chief Jefferson sighed. "Well, then, all I can say is

that you were very lucky. On a windy night like tonight, a fire can get out of control in no time."

Mr. and Mrs. Brown and their daughters nodded solemnly. They knew that they had had a very close call.

"So, what happened?" Chief Jefferson asked. "Did you smell the smoke?"

The Browns shook their heads.

"We were all asleep," Mrs. Brown said.

Chief Jefferson frowned. "Then I don't understand what happened. Who woke you up?"

The Browns looked at one another.

"It was Santa Paws!" they all said in unison. "Who else?"

It was Christmas morning, and the Callahans were getting ready to go to church. On Christmas Eve, they had gone over to the Oceanport Hospital maternity ward to visit their brand-new niece. Mr. Callahan's brother Steve and his wife, Emily, had had a beautiful baby girl named Miranda. Gregory and Patricia thought she was kind of red and wrinkly, but on the whole, pretty cute.

On the way home, they talked their parents into stopping at the middle school. But when they went to the little alcove, the food and water dishes hadn't been touched. The towels were still neatly folded, too. For some reason, the dog had never returned. Maybe he was gone for good.

Gregory knew that something terrible must have happened to him, but right now, there wasn't anything he could do about it. As far as he knew, no one had seen the dog since he had found Rachel's wallet that morning. And that was *hours* ago. Now, for all Gregory knew, the dog could be lying somewhere, alone, and scared, and *hurt*.

His father put his hand on his shoulder. "Come on, Greg," he said gently. "It'll be okay. We'll come back again tomorrow."

Gregory nodded, and followed his family back to the car.

They went home and ate cookies and listened to Christmas carols. Mrs. Callahan made popcorn. Mr. Callahan read *The Night Before Christmas* aloud. Patricia told complicated jokes, and Gregory pretended that he thought they were funny. Then they all went to bed.

Gregory didn't get much sleep. He was too upset. Deep inside, he knew that the dog was gone for good. He was sure that he would never see him again — and the thought of that made him feel like crying.

Santa Paws

When he got up, even though it was Christmas Day, he was more sad than excited. He and his father both put on suits and ties to wear to church. His mother and Patricia wore long skirts and festive blouses. Patricia also braided red and green ribbons into her hair.

Every year, on Christmas morning, there was a special, nonreligious, interdenominational service in Oceanport. No matter what holiday they celebrated, everyone in town was invited. This year, the service was being held at the Catholic church, but Rabbi Gladstone was going to be the main speaker. Next year, the service would be held at the Baptist church, and the Methodist minister would lead the ceremony. As Father Reilly always said, it wasn't about religion, it was about *community*. It was about *neighbors*.

"Come on, Gregory," Mrs. Callahan said as they got into the station wagon. "Cheer up. It's Christmas."

Gregory nodded, and did his best to smile. Inside, though, he was miserable.

"When we get home, we have all those presents to open," Patricia reminded him. "And I spent *a lot* of money on yours."

Gregory smiled, feebly.

Santa Paws

The church was very crowded. Almost the entire town had shown up. People were smiling, and waving, and shaking hands with each other. There was a definite feeling of goodwill in the air. Oceanport was *always* a friendly and tolerant town, but the holiday season was special.

Gregory sat in his family's pew with his eyes closed and his hands tightly folded. He was wishing with all of his heart that the dog was okay. No matter how hard he tried, he couldn't seem to feel *any* Christmas spirit. How could he believe in the magic of Christmas, if he couldn't even save one little stray dog?

Rabbi Gladstone stepped up to the podium in the front of the church. "Welcome, everyone," he said. "Season's greetings to all of you!"

Then, the service began.

After the fire had been put out and the Browns had gone across the street to stay with the neighbors, the dog was alone underneath his bush. He dragged himself deeper into the woods, whimpering softly. He knew he was badly hurt, and that he needed help.

He crawled through the woods until he couldn't make it any further. Then he lay down on his side in the snow. He stayed in that same position all night long. By now, he was too exhausted even to *whimper*.

In the morning, he made himself get up. If he stayed here by himself, he might die. Somehow, he had to make it back to the school. If he could do that, maybe his friends Gregory and Oscar would come and help him. He *needed* help, desperately.

Each limping step was harder than the one before, and the dog had to force himself to keep going. The town seemed to be deserted. He limped down Main Street, undisturbed.

The park was empty, too. The dog staggered across the wide expanse, falling down more than once. He was cold, he was in pain, and he was *exhausted*.

Naturally, he was also hungry.

When he tottered past the church, he paused at the bottom of the stairs. The doors were open and welcoming, warm air rushed out at him. For days, he had been trying to *give* help. Maybe now it was time to *get* some.

He dragged himself up to the steps. His shoulder throbbed and burned with pain the entire way. When he got to the top, he was panting heavily. Could he make it any further, or should he just fall down right here?

He could smell lots of people. Too many people. Too many different scents. Some of the scents were familiar, but he was too confused to sort them all out. *Walking* took up all of his energy.

He hobbled into the church, weaving from side to side. He started down the center aisle, and then his bad leg gave out under his weight. He fell on the floor and then couldn't get up again. He let his head slump forward against his front paws and then closed his eyes.

A hush fell over the church.

"I don't believe it," someone said, sounding stunned. "It's Santa Paws!"

Now that the silence had been broken, everyone started talking at once.

Hearing the name "Santa Paws," Gregory sat up straight in his pew. Then he stood up so he could see better.

"That's my dog," he whispered, so excited that he was barely able to breathe. "Look at my poor dog!" Then he put his pinkies in his mouth and let out — noisy *air*.

Sitting next to him, Patricia sighed deeply. "*Really*, Greg," she said, and shook her head with grave disappointment. "Is that the best you can do?" She sighed again. Then she stuck her fingers in her mouth, and sent out a sharp, clear, and *earsplitting* whistle.

Instantly, the dog lifted his head. His ears shot up, and his tail began to rise.

"That's my dog!" Gregory shouted. He climbed past his parents and stumbled out into the aisle.

The dog was still too weak to get up, but he waved his tail as Gregory ran over to him.

"Are you all right?" Gregory asked, fighting back tears. "Don't worry, I'll take care of you. You're safe now."

Everyone in the church started yelling at once and trying to crowd around the injured dog.

Patricia lifted her party skirt up a few inches so that she wouldn't trip on it. Then she stepped delicately into the aisle on her bright red holiday high heels.

"Quiet, please," she said in her most commanding voice. Then she raised her hands for silence. "Is there a veterinarian in the house?"

A man and a woman sitting in different sections of the church each stood up.

"Good." Patricia motioned for them both to come forward. "Step aside, please, everyone, and let them through."

A few people did as she said, but there was still a

large, concerned group hovering around Gregory and the dog. The veterinarians were trying to get through, but the aisle was jammed.

Patricia's whistle was even more piercing this time. "I *said*," she repeated herself in a no-nonsense voice, "please step aside, in an orderly fashion."

The people standing in this aisle meekly did as they were told.

Watching all of this from their pew, Mr. Callahan leaned over to his wife.

"Do you get the sudden, sinking feeling that some-day we're going to have another cop in the family?" he asked.

Mrs. Callahan laughed. "I've had that feeling since she was *two*," she answered.

Gregory waited nervously as the two veterinari-ans examined the dog.

"Don't worry," the female vet announced after a couple of minutes. "He's going to be just fine."

Her colleague nodded. "Once we get him cleaned up and bandaged, and put in a few stitches, he'll be as good as new!"

Everyone in the church started clapping.

"Hooray for Santa Paws!" someone yelled.

"Merry Christmas, and God bless us everyone!" a little boy in the front row contributed.

Santa Paws

Mr. Callahan leaned over to his wife again. "If that kid is holding a crutch, I'm *out* of here."

Mrs. Callahan grinned. "That's just Nathaniel Haversham. His parents are *actors*."

"Oh." Mr. Callahan looked relieved. "Good."

Up in the front of the church, Rabbi Gladstone tapped on the microphone to get everyone's attention. Gradually, the church quieted down.

"Thank you," he said. "I think that this week, we've all seen proof that there *can* be holiday miracles. Even when it's hard to believe in magic, wonderful, unexplained things can still happen. That dog — an ordinary dog — has been saving lives and helping people throughout this season." He smiled in the dog's direction. "Thank you, and welcome to Oceanport, Santa Paws!"

Gregory didn't want to be rude, but he had to speak up. "Um, I'm sorry, Rabbi, but that's not his name," he said shyly.

"Whew," Patricia said, and pretended to wipe her arm across her forehead. "Promise me you're not going to call him Brownie, or Muffin, or anything else *cute*."

Gregory nodded. If he came up with a cute name, his sister would never let him live it down. Somehow, the name would have to be *cool*.

"What is his name, son?" Rabbi Gladstone asked kindly from the podium.

Gregory blinked a few times. His mind was a complete blank. "Well, uh, it's uh —"

"Sparky!" Oscar shouted, sitting with his family several rows away.

Everyone laughed.

"It's *not* Sparky," Gregory assured them. "It's, uh —"

"Solomon's a very nice name," Rabbi Gladstone suggested. "Isaiah has a nice ring to it, too."

Now, everyone in the church started shouting out different ideas. Names like Hero, and Rex, and Buttons.

"Oh, yeah, *Buttons*," Patricia said under her breath. "Like we wouldn't be totally humiliated to have a dog named *Buttons*."

Other names were suggested. Champ, and Sport, and Dasher, and Dancer. Frank, and Foxy, and Bud.

Bud?

Gregory looked at his dog for a long time. The dog wagged his tail and then lifted his paw into his new owner's lap. Gregory thought some more, and then, out of nowhere, it came to him. After all, what was another name for Santa Claus?

"His name's Nicholas," he told everyone. Then he

_ı proudly and shook the dog's paw. "We'll call ın _Nick_."

The dog barked and wagged his tail.

Then, Gregory stood up, "Come on, Nicky," he said. "It's time to go home."

The dog got up, too, balancing on three legs. He wagged his tail as hard as he could, and pressed his muzzle into Gregory's hand. He had a new owner, he had a new home, and he was going to have a whole new life.

He could hardly wait to get started!